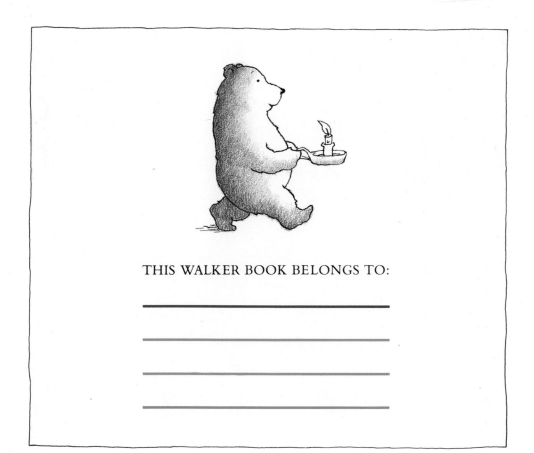

THIS WALKER BOOK BELONGS TO:

For Alice and Melissa (Laura)

First published 1992
by Walker Books Ltd
87 Vauxhall Walk
London SE11 5HJ

This edition published 1994

2 4 6 8 10 9 7 5 3 1

© 1992 Penny Dale

Printed in Hong Kong

British Library Cataloguing in Publication Data
A catalogue record for this book is available
from the British Library.

ISBN 0-7445-3164-0

ALL ABOUT
Alice

PENNY DALE

WALKER BOOKS
LONDON

Alice was getting dressed. So was her big sister Laura.

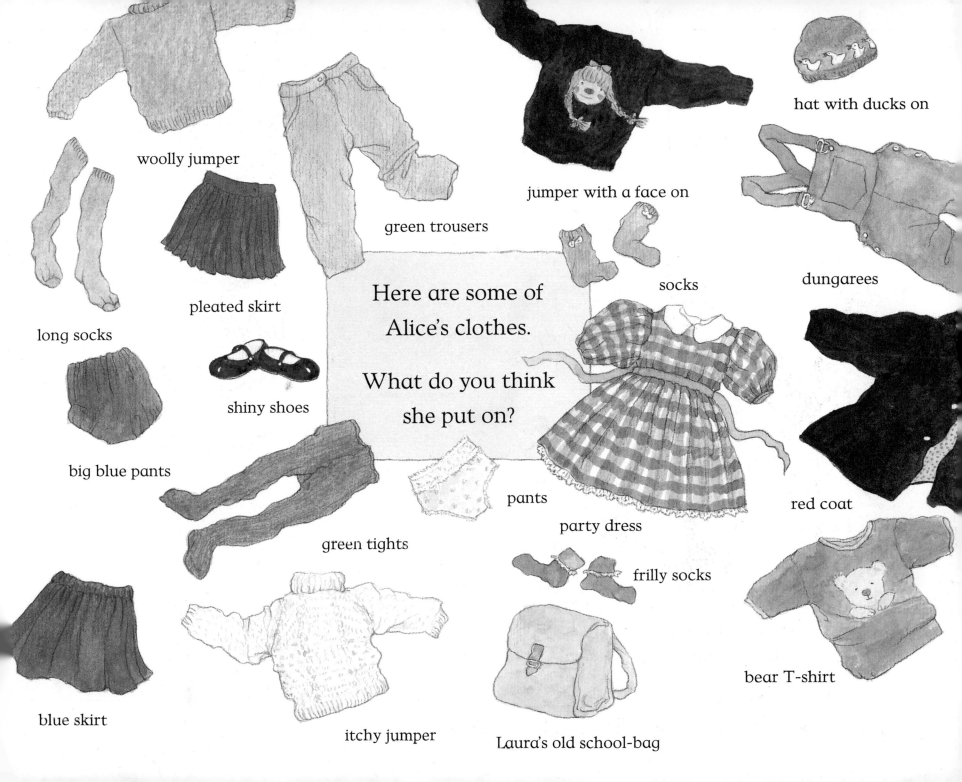

woolly jumper

hat with ducks on

jumper with a face on

green trousers

dungarees

long socks

pleated skirt

socks

Here are some of
Alice's clothes.

What do you think
she put on?

shiny shoes

big blue pants

green tights

pants

party dress

red coat

frilly socks

blue skirt

itchy jumper

Laura's old school-bag

bear T-shirt

Alice put on her jumper with a face on, her green trousers, her blue skirt, her hat with ducks, and Laura's old school-bag.

Then Dad came in and helped her dress properly and took her down to breakfast.

apple

bread and jam

milk

cheese

raisins

egg with soldiers

What do you think
Alice had for breakfast?

toast

raisins

banana

orange

cereal

yoghurt

biscuits

Alice had cereal for breakfast, but she didn't eat it.
Alice wanted her sister's breakfast.

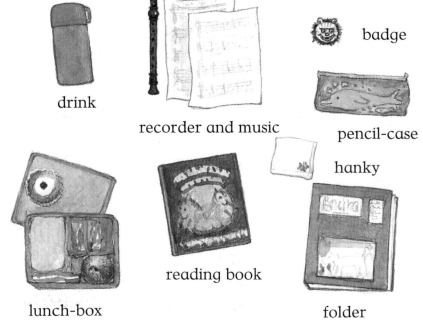

drink

recorder and music

badge

pencil-case

hanky

lunch-box

reading book

folder

...akfast Laura packed her school-bag. This is what she put in it.

crayons

old raisins

leaves

Laura's cake

scrumpled
paper

scarf

Alice packed her
school-bag too.

What do you think
she put in it?

car

jewels

pink recorder

crusts

monkey

bits of
cereal

book

lump of coal

twigs

old sweet

Alice put everything in her school-bag, except her monkey and her sister's cake.

She carried her monkey and gave back the cake.

Mum, Alice and Laura walked to school.

In the playground Alice started crying. Why do you think Alice cried?

Alice cried because the big children went into school without her.
She was too young to go to school.

Mum and Alice walked home.

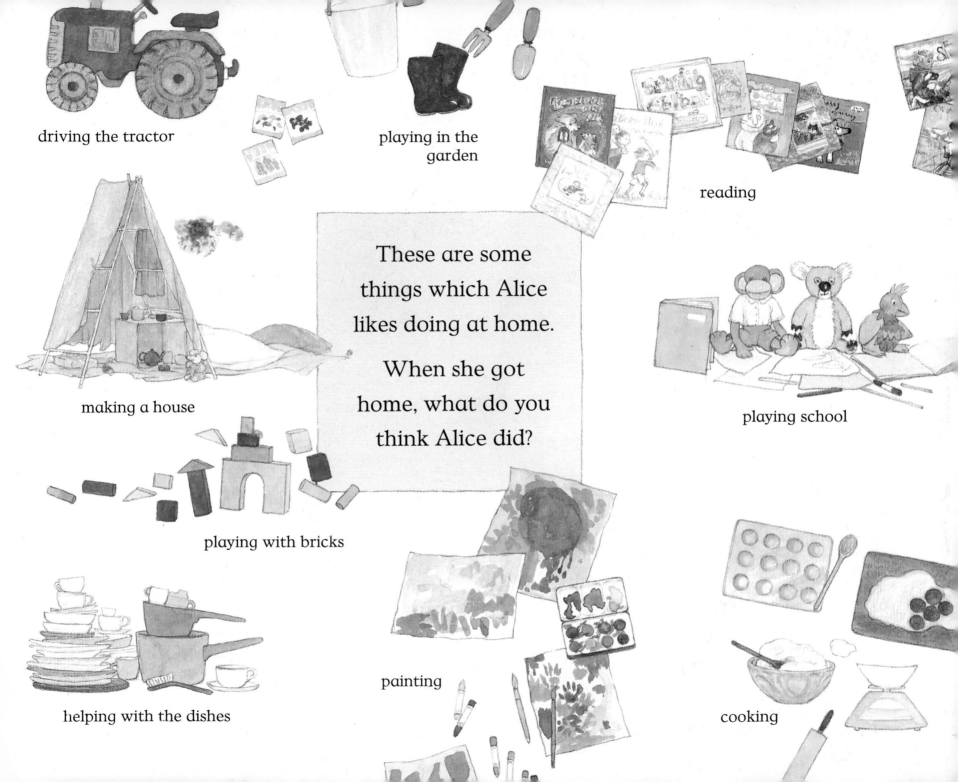

driving the tractor

playing in the garden

reading

making a house

playing school

These are some things which Alice likes doing at home.

When she got home, what do you think Alice did?

playing with bricks

painting

cooking

helping with the dishes

At home Alice went straight upstairs to play school.

She went out in the garden and found a spider.

She did some painting and cooking and reading. She helped with the dishes.

two sandwiches

one small tomato

three pieces of cheese

twenty-seven crisps

half a yoghurt

four slices of cucumber

one big apple

her cake like Laura's

At lunch-time Alice had a picnic in the garden. This is what she ate.

After lunch Alice made a house and drove the tractor round the garden.

She went back upstairs to play school, and then it was time for a rest.

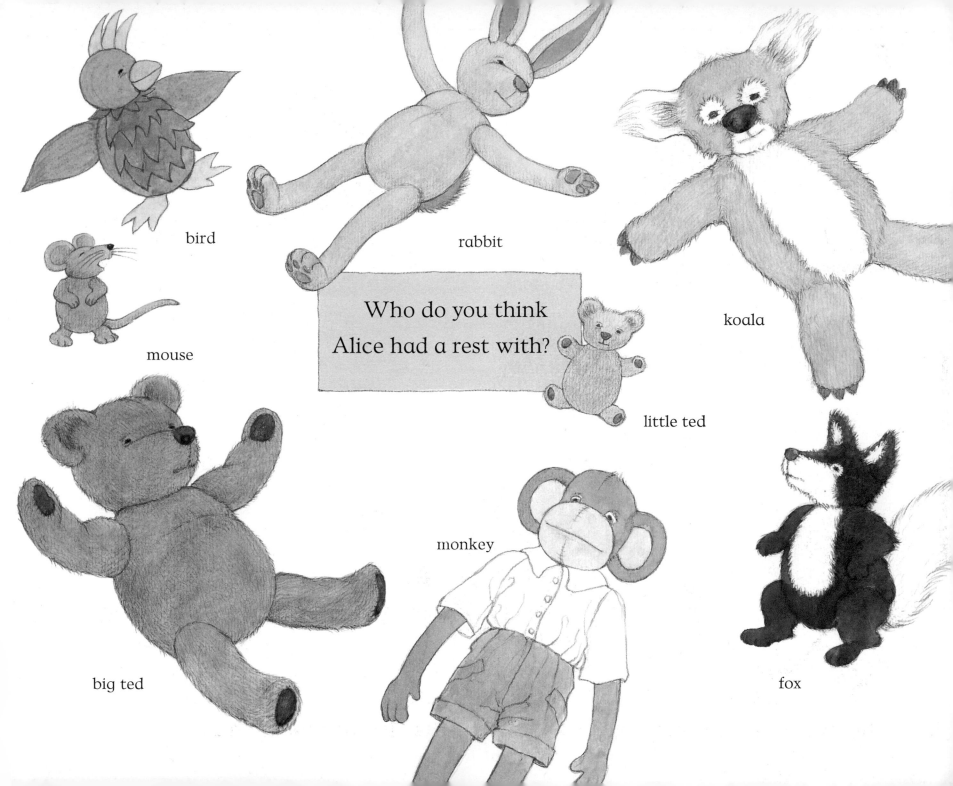

bird

rabbit

koala

mouse

Who do you think
Alice had a rest with?

little ted

big ted

monkey

fox

Alice rested with all the animals.

Mum woke Alice when it was time to fetch Laura from school. Alice was cross at first.

But soon she was smiling again. Why do you think she was smiling?

Alice was smiling because she knew the big children were about to come out of school

After school Alice played with Amy and the twins. Then it was time to go home.

Can you see Laura?

What do you think Alice did all the way home?

All the way home Alice copied her sister.

When they got home Alice went on copying her sister.
She copied her playing the recorder. She copied her watching TV.

She copied her going upstairs. What do you think happened
when Laura went into their room?

When Laura went into their room, she was cross with Alice because of the mess.
She said she wanted to play on her own and collected up her things.

Alice played on her own too. But she didn't collect up her things, she got more out.

tie-on wings

dressing-up clothes

old decorations

Here are the things
Alice got out.

What do you think
happened next?

masks

face paints

hats

Alice got dressed up. Then the twins and Amy came round.

Everyone got dressed up like Alice . . .

and ran out into the garden to play.

MORE WALKER PAPERBACKS
For You to Enjoy
Also by Penny Dale

PLAY WITH ALICE AND LAURA

Using the press-outs in this book, you can help Alice and Laura choose what to wear,
what to eat and what games to play – then put them to bed with their favourite toy animals!

0-7445-2558-6   £4.99

BET YOU CAN'T!

"A lively argumentative dialogue – using simple, repetitive words – between two children.
Illustrated with great humour and realism." *Practical Parenting*

0-7445-1225-5   £3.99

WAKE UP, MR. B!

Commended for the Kate Greenaway Medal, this is the simple account of a small
girl playing some imaginative early morning games with her dog.

"Perceptive, domestic illustrations fill a varied cartoon-strip format … making
this a lovely tell-it-yourself picture book." *The Good Book Guide*

0-7445-1467-3   £3.99

TEN IN THE BED

"A subtle variation on the traditional nursery song, illustrated with wonderfully
warm pictures … crammed with amusing details." *Practical Parenting*

0-7445-1340-5   £3.99

**Walker Paperbacks are available from most booksellers, or by post from
Walker Books Ltd, PO Box 11, Falmouth, Cornwall TR10 9EN.**

To order, send: Title, author, ISBN number and price for each book ordered, your full name and address,
cheque or postal order for the total amount, plus postage and packing:

UK and BFPO Customers – £1.00 for first book, plus 50p for the second book and plus 30p for each additional book to a maximum charge of £3.00.
Overseas and Eire Customers – £2.00 for first book, plus £1.00 for the second book and plus 50p per copy for each additional book.
Prices are correct at time of going to press, but are subject to change without notice.